A BEAUMONT SERIES NOVELLA

Edited by Fallon Clark at SnowEditing.com
Cover Designed by Sarah Hansen at OkayCreations.net

ISBN: 978-0-615-78808-1

Contents

Chapter 1

She's everything I'm not looking for yet each day when I return, she's there, greeting me with the warmest smile, the softest touch and expecting nothing but hospitality in return; and each night I lie in my bunk and think of her. I imagine what it would feel like to run my fingers through her sun-bleached hair. I close my eyes and picture myself holding her tight, our bare skin touching, our lips connecting. I tell myself that tomorrow will be the day. Tomorrow I'll walk into work and, instead of taking my charts from her, I'll ask her to dinner. I'll ask her to take a walk with me at lunchtime. Anything to get us away from the clinic and allow us to be adults for one moment before the hectic day bombards us with agony and despair.

Each morning I wake, prepared to start the day as I had planned, and fail. When I look at the picture that sits on top of my nightstand I'm reminded why I'm here.

No matter how many days, weeks, months pass, things have not gotten easier. The way I left Beaumont haunts me. I was a coward. I was a grown man in an adult relationship – one that was raising a child – and instead of staying and fighting for my family, I allowed someone to walk in and take it away.

I knew I had a fight on my hands when the doors swung open and he was behind Katelyn. I thought for sure that if he ever came back she would be on my side, but actually seeing her with him, I knew. My life flashed before my eyes. The only problem was that instead of me with Noah, it was Liam, and I was standing on the outside. It didn't matter if Josie was on my arm; deep down I knew she was going to be wherever Liam was.

I tried so hard to be the bigger man and I failed. I thought I could make it work. I could be the bona fide stepdad and we'd be a happy family. Josie and I would finally get married and Noah could visit Liam on alternating weekends and holidays. I had it all planned out in my head. Late at night when I'd wake and find that she wasn't in our bed, all I could do was think. Think about how it was going to fall on me to make sure everyone was happy. Think about how in the blink of an eye I was losing everything and did nothing to deserve what was happening.

Instead, I left. I walked away from my practice and my life without a goodbye and now I live with regret. I should've never walked out on Noah's life the way I did. He didn't deserve that. For years I was his father figure. His football and baseball coach, his study partner. He was my go-to guy when I wanted to do something special for Josie, my right-hand man, and I left him. I never once considered his feelings. Even though he has Liam, we had something special. Each day that I think about it is a reminder that he's the only person with whom I need to make amends for my actions.

I watch as she leaves for work. She doesn't even look away from her car. If she had she'd see me sitting out here watching her. I hoped she'd stay home today and we could talk. We could fix things and figure out how we're going to make it.

She drives away, oblivious to her surroundings. It pains me to see her like this. When did I not matter to her anymore?

I pull into the driveway and park. This will be the last time I'm here. I stare at the house and see all the happy times we spent outside, landscaping the yard. The hours I spent teaching Noah how to throw a football and baseball. The nights under the floodlights where we'd shoot free throws. Memories. That is all I have from the last six years.

I let myself in the house and look around. I think I was secretly expecting things to be different when I walked in. Maybe I was hoping to see that she was moving on without me, but everything is the same. My football bag is where I threw it last night. Her afghan is spread across the couch, her new bed. My heart breaks thinking that she didn't sleep in our bed last night even though I wasn't here. It's as if she thinks it's tainted.

I go out to the garage and get a few boxes. It's sad to think I've lived here for the past five years and all my stuff can fit in a few boxes. Nothing in this house belongs to me. That should've been my first clue. I should've pushed for us to get a new house, make a new home for us, but I was afraid to rock the boat. I shouldn't have lived that like. It' wasn't fair to her or me.

With the boxes in hand, I start in the bedroom. My bathroom essentials are easily packed in an overnight bag. I bring out my suitcase and pack my clothes, clearing out my side of the closet.

I try not to get emotional when packing, but lose it when I come across the engagement ring I bought her, but never found the time to slip onto her finger. Maybe if I had, she'd be here with me now. I can't believe I was so stupid.

I finish packing, stopping in Noah's room. I just need to look around and feel his presence. I'm going to miss him. I run back to the bedroom and take the picture of Noah sitting on the dresser and take it with me. It's not enough, but it will have to do since I won't be in his life anymore.

He must hate me. He should. I hate myself for walking out on him, but I have no doubt he's being well taken care of. Liam, with his never-ending bank account, and Josie – the most resilient woman I know – leave no question in my mind that Noah is well cared for and that's all I can ask.

I should call. I've tried. I've picked up the phone a few times and dialed their number only to hang up before it rings. I guess I don't want to know if they're still living in her house, the house we shared as family. I don't want to know that she's moved on and erased the happy memories that we all shared. I'm not sure how I'd deal with that knowledge. Some things are better left unknown.

I dress in my usual khaki shorts and an Under Armour polo shirt and slip on my worn-out Nikes. I'm going to need to order some new clothes soon; these have seen better days. The dirt and harsh water really do a number on your clothes after a while. The walk to the clinic from our dorm is short and, for me, a luxury. It gives me ample time to converse with the residents and greet the children as they do their daily chores.

My life as a doctor is fulfilling, but it wasn't until I came to Africa that I finally found peace with who I am as an individual. The people here are beyond grateful for anything that I can do for them and I am indebted to them simply because they trust me with their most precious commodity – their children.

The temperature doesn't change when I walk into the clinic. The air inside is just as stifling as out, but with the added smell of antiseptic. Aubrey, our newest staff member, has her back turned to me. I take a moment and look her over. I've tried not to stare like the other doctors, but it's hard not to. She's been the subject of my dreams lately, even though I try not to think about her in that way. It's hard not to gawk. She's one of those natural beauties that other women strive to look like. I know a few of Josie and Katelyn's friends pay a lot of money to have Aubrey's blond hair. Her eyes, blue like the ocean, are full of life when she smiles.

I shouldn't be attracted to her. It's wrong. She's my co-worker and a friend, and I can't afford to be anything more to her. I watch as she talks to one of the other nurses. She throws her head back and laughs and I wish I knew what they were talking about.

From the day that Aubrey arrived, I tried not to be in the same room with her but it was unavoidable. We work together a lot and it's the subtle brushes of our skin when we pass over a patient, the coy looks and shy smiles that make my knees buckle. She's nothing like Josie. Aubrey is petite, barely five foot three. I must look like the Jolly Green Giant standing next to her.

Aubrey turns toward the waiting room and sees me. Her reaction is instant. I don't even need to look past her flirtatious eyes; they tell me everything I need to know. I try not to act shy, but I fail miserably. My head moves on its own volition as it turns slightly downward. I smile back and am rewarded with the most beautiful shade of pink when she blushes. In this moment, her smile is my salvation.

I know she's from South Africa. Her parents are American missionaries but she was born and raised here. I never see her with make-up or her hair full of products. Her bright blue eyes accent her lightly sun-kissed skin. I should take the time to get to know her. If anything, she can at least be a friend.

I take the pile of charts from her extended hand and hold them to my chest, a move simply to protect my most valuable asset, one that needs to heal and be whole again.

I nod and walk back to my makeshift office. A thin piece of gauzy fabric creates the walls we use around here. When I first arrived, my expectations were so low that I was pleasantly surprised at what I'd be working with. Albeit, it's not much, but it's enough for me to provide good healthcare for the patients and it's more than enough for me to get my mind off of things back home.

My day is relatively smooth, peaceful even. I see a few of my favorite kids and they coax me into a game of football after work. I can't pass up the opportunity to spend time with them; it's one of the reasons I'm here.

When I told Josie we were moving, I knew she wouldn't come with me. It was my last-ditch effort to save what was falling through my fingers. I won't lie, I saw Noah out there playing with these children and appreciating what he had, giving him the ability to teach them what he knew and learn from them. For me it was a win-win. I'd be doing a service as a doctor and a parent. I was being selfish.

After handing Aubrey my files and once again avoiding any personal contact, I step outside into the blazing inferno. Nightfall will be a welcome reprieve simply because the sun won't be burning itself into our skin.

"Doctor, doctor," one of my young patients yells. He's motioning for me to come to him. He kicks his football to his buddy and takes my hand, pulling me into the circle. He tells his friends that I'm playing—this much I can decipher as the kids split off into two teams.

I crawl into bed and pull her into my arms. She's so warm and soft against my rough hands. Tomorrow is our two-year anniversary. I have plans that I've kept secret from her. I had to work out the logistics with her parents so they could watch Noah and her mom can work in the store. I've been on her about hiring someone, but she's happy working alone.

"Are you asleep?" I whisper against her skin.

"Mhm," she mumbles.

"Liar."

She rolls in my arms, her fingertips dancing along the stubble on my jaw. I lean down and kiss her softly.

"I love you, Josie."

"I love you too."

"Noah wants to play football. He asked me after dinner." I feel her stiffen in my arms. I wish I could take away the pain, but she never talks about it. I hate that she has to deal with all this shit. Sometimes I wish Noah was a girl. Maybe things would be different.

I know she sees Liam when she looks at Noah. Hell, I do. It's like Liam is living in our house while not actually being here.

"I don't want him playing."

"I know you don't, but he's a boy and his friends are playing. It's a natural thing for him to want to play. Plus, there's Mason. We are throwing football down his throat."

She rests her head on my chest, her fingers dancing along my skin. "He can't turn out like his dad."

"He won't. I won't let it go to his head."

"You'll protect him?"

"As if he were my own, Josie. You should know that."

"Okay."

"Okay," I say, kissing the top of her head. She knew this day was coming and I know she was hoping he'd play soccer. We'll just have to deal with it.

I quickly realize that I'm the only one with a shirt on, so I strip mine off and match the boys. They giggle relentlessly at the white man standing in front of them so I do what any self-respecting man would do; I steal the ball and dribble toward their goal. The laughing quickly stops when they figure out what I'm trying to do and now we have a game.

It isn't long until it's time for the children to head to their homes. I hug them all goodbye with promises of another rematch. This is probably the best workout I've had since I arrived and something I'll definitely do again. The bonding is important so that they trust me. I need for them to know that I'm an okay person even if sometimes I have to give them shots.

I bend to pick up my dust-covered shirt and my eyes land on Aubrey. She's standing in the doorway of the clinic, watching us. For the first time I wave and watch in amazement as her face lights up. She waves back and stands a little straighter. I don't know what I'm doing here. With Josie, everything progressed naturally. She brought Noah in shortly after I took over the practice and I saw how lonely she looked. I took a chance that night and brought them dinner, determined to shower them both with love and affection, not just her. I wanted both of them to be in my life. I was bold then and look where it got me.

I shake the dust out of my shirt but don't put it back on. I'm sweaty, it's dirty and I'm in desperate need of a shower. I take a step forward, not really sure where I'm going, but hope is written all over her face. She wants me to talk to her and I have no reason not to oblige.

She meets me half way, out on the dirt road that is also the children's playground. There is an air about her, a calmness that surrounds her. Here she is, tending to the needy when she could've escaped to the comforts of America.

"You're not half bad." Her accent, something I've never really paid attention to, catches me off guard. She speaks perfect English, but it's refined and educated. Not something I expect from a missionary's daughter.

"They're trying to kill me." I say as if I'm out of breath, which is ridiculous because I've had time to settle myself. Does she make me nervous? It's been years since I've been nervous around a woman. Not even Josie made me nervous. I was content with her, until I asked her to marry me.

"They were having fun with you. It's nice to see. Many times doctors only come to work. They do their jobs and retire to their huts for the night and ignore what is going on around them. But you're different."

Is being different good? I want to think it is. I never want to go through life being the same as someone else. I've always wanted to be unique, genuine. I want to be remembered and make an impression on people.

"Anything to see them smile," I say and realize that I really want to see her smile again. She's eye-catching and deserves to be on the cover of magazines. Her beauty is pure and unharnessed and I shudder at the thought of her glamming herself up for an event. I would be one lucky bastard to have her grace my side as a date sometime.

I roll my eyes at the thought. She's a co-worker and we're advised not to get too attached because we can switch locations at any given time and, with communications the way they are here, keeping in touch is just about impossible.

"Would you like to get something to eat?" I slap my hand to my forehead. That was stupid. Not asking her out because that seemed normal, but the 'something to eat' part. It's not like we can drive down to the nearest diner and eat a decent meal.

"I'd love to," she responds. I pull my hand away, noticing that she's not kidding. Her eyes are expressive, telling me that she wants this.

I look around, clearly trying to make restaurants and markets appear out of thin air. I shrug and shake my head. "I think my mouth got the better of me. I'm not sure where to take you."

She laughs and it's the most melodic sound I've ever heard. "Tell you what, Dr. Ashford, you go take a shower and when you're done, you can come to my place. I'll make us something to eat."

I look up and down the road and start laughing. How romantic will it be to eat in the mess hall of our humble abode?

"Your place, huh?"

She nods, clearly excited. "Yes, I have a very spacious kitchen where we can stretch out and not feel cramped as if we were in a tiny bistro on the streets of Italy."

I chuckle and give her kudos for her wicked imagination. She gives me an idea and for the first time I think I want to try something.

"Tell you what. You get dinner ready and I'll meet you in your fancy kitchen. But we'll eat someplace else."

She looks at me, fear evident in her eyes. We all know it's not safe to be out at night, but I would never do anything to put her in harm's way.

"Don't worry," I say as I touch her arm. I don't mean to, but now that I have I can't let go. I look from her to my hand and back to her. She's looking at my hand and I can't tell if she's disgusted or pleased. Either way, I have to let go because I'm not prepared to handle the tingling sensation I'm getting from touching her.

"I'm going to go shower," I say, stepping away from her. I hate leaving her in the middle of the road, but if I stay, I fear verbal vomit will get the best of me and I don't want to scare her off. I'm scared enough for the both of us.

Chapter 2

The cold water is a welcome reprieve. For the most part, I enjoy the cold trickle, but there are times when a hot shower would do to ease my aches and pains. Hot water is a rare luxury around here. Before I arrived, I spent a week in a hotel in Florida on the beach. This was the hotel where Josie and I were supposed to go on vacation. The night before we were to leave, we fought. It was the first time since we'd been together that I was glad that Noah wasn't there. I needed to say some things and didn't want him to hear me.

Instead of us packing for our vacation, we were breaking up. I was breaking us up, beating her to the inevitable. I have no doubt she would've stayed with me out of obligation, but I couldn't put her in that position. In the back of my mind, she would've cheated and that is the one thing I couldn't live with. I know her that well to know she was second-guessing us.

Once Mason passed away I knew things would change. I fully expected to step up and help Katelyn with the girls. What I didn't expect was for Liam to return. I would've never thought that he kept tabs on everyone, or even read the paper. What were the chances that he read it the day after Mason was killed?

I work my neck muscles under the water. I want to stop thinking about my life in Beaumont. I don't want to know what's going on there. How Peyton and Elle are doing and whether Katelyn has taken them to see a therapist. They need it, whether she is willing to admit it or not. She needs it, too. She spent far too much time consoling Josie than she did dealing with her husband's death. I chide myself for not sticking around at least for her and the twins.

I shut off the water and wrap a towel around my waist. There is no need to dry off; the heat will do the job. My clothes selection is limited, but given that I live in a dust bowl and an oven, the fewer clothes the better. Except for the bugs. I could do without the killer mosquitoes and constantly sleeping under a net.

I dress quickly again in khaki shorts and opt for a black dress shirt. I don't know why I brought it; it's not like I have fancy dinners or meetings to attend. The dress attire here is causal and relaxed. No stuffy doctors coats or gaudy nurses uniforms staring at us all day.

I run down to our reading room and grab the small card table and two folding chairs and take them out back. We have a small deck area, but nothing to sit on. I set up the table and chairs, wishing I had a candle or a vase of flowers to add to the ambiance. This will have to do.

Aubrey is standing in the kitchen with two plates and two glasses of water in front of her. Her grin is infectious and I can't help the wide smile that cracks over my own face. My stride is quick as I make my way to where she's standing and even though she's in shorts and t-shirt, similar to what she wore today to work, I take in all of her.

I pick up the plates of food and signal for her to follow me. She gasps when we step outside. I know it's not much and if we were home I could offer her better, but we're here and I'm trying to make this the best first date either of us are going to have in Africa.

First date? Did I mean to call what we are doing here tonight a date? Many colleagues meet and have tea or share a dinner. Why classify what we are doing as a date? Is it because deep down this is what I want?

Setting the plates down, I pull out the chair for her and help her scoot under the table. I watch as she puts the napkin on her lap. I sit across from her and do the same. Everything feels comfortable, like she and I have been doing this for years, yet I know nothing about her.

"So, Dr. Ashford, how are you liking Africa?" She doesn't waste any time. I thought we'd eat a bit before we delved into personal talk.

I rest my arms on the table and look at her so she knows I'm giving her my full attention.

"Please, call me Nick. And I like it here, for the most part. There are things that I miss from home, like air conditioning…" I laugh. "I miss other things too, but nothing material. What about you? This has to be different from South Africa."

Aubrey sets her spoon down and puts her hands in her lap. "My parents, they wanted the best for me. They may be missionaries and I went to boarding school, but I spent my summers in their camps. They wanted me to experience both worlds and decide for myself what I wanted to do."

"And what did you decide?"

"I haven't yet. I'm supposed to start college in the fall. I've taken a year off to volunteer."

The word college catches my attention. I mentally take a step back. I never gave age a consideration. I know I've checked out of the conversation. She's still talking, but I don't hear a world she's saying.

Her fingers snap in front of my face. I have to blink a few times to bring myself back into this realm.

"Is it something I said?"

"No," I lie.

"Okay." I can see the hurt on her face and I feel like a total shit. What the hell is wrong with me? Here I am sitting across from a beautiful woman and I'm worried about her age. Why does that even matter?

"Aubrey, I'm sorry. I was taken aback by your college remark."

"Oh." I can't tell if she's relieved or just accepting that I'm nothing but a jerk.

"Can I ask how old you are?"

Aubrey takes a drink of her water. There's a wicked glint in her when she puts her glass down. "I'm twenty-one and have probably seen and experienced more in my lifetime than you ever will."

"You're right," I say.

I need to fix this. I need to stop being stupid and letting something as trivial as age affect me. I throw my napkin down on the table and push my chair back. Her face falls and it's in that moment that I know I can do this. That is what I tell myself as I reach for the plates. I can be a man and start living my life whether it's here or back home. I can live with my turmoil over Noah while letting my life take a different course. Is that course with Aubrey? I don't know. What I do know is that I don't like the way she looked when I stood up.

"I'm not very hungry. Would you like to go for a walk?"

She looks up at me and nods. We clean up our mess, washing and putting away our dishes, and make our way out of the dorm. We walk to the edge of the compound and as much as I'd love to leave, we don't. There is enough to explore without compromising our safety.

I direct us toward the playground. The children are all in for the night so we have some privacy. She sits on the swing and I take this opportunity to stand behind her. I push her gently and watch as she sways back and forth. I remember doing this with Noah when he was little, teaching him how to pump his legs in and out. He outgrew swinging the moment he picked up a football. I saw the talent in him, but wanted to ignore it. I didn't want Josie having to deal with what she hated most in her life, but as his parents, we couldn't pretend it wasn't happening. I did the next best thing and started coaching Noah and instilled as many values as I could.

"I'm sorry for my reaction back there. I'm here…I'm here because my fiancée and I broke up and this was the best way for me to deal with it. Initially, I had hoped she was going to come with me, but things didn't work out that way."

"Are you still in love with her?" Aubrey's voice is quiet, serene.

I think about her question and roll it over in my head. Am I still in love with Josie? I don't know.

I never thought I'd see her again. We didn't stay in touch when I went off to college, not that we had any reason to, but it would've been nice. I look down at the chart in my hand and see the name: Noah. I look back at her. She smiles weakly as the toddler in her arms cries uncontrollably. She looks tired and rightfully so.

"Josephine, it's good to see you," I say in my doctor voice. I had such a crush on her in high school, but she wouldn't give me the time of

day. She was always with Liam Westbury, even though she could do so much better than him.

"Josie," she replies. I nod, remembering that she didn't like anyone to use her first name.

"You have a son?" I don't mean for my words to come out as a question, but I'm shocked. I look at the file and see his name is Preston and not Westbury. My brow furrows, but I can't ask her the question on my mind.

"I do and he's sick and I don't know what's wrong with him." She breaks down in tears. I get up and take the baby from her arms and lay him down on the table. He screams louder and tugs at his ear.

I look into his offending ear with my otoscope and see the irritation. I move my hands over his neck, shoulders and stomach feeling for any other issues to determine if we are working strictly with an ear infection or something else.

"I'll be right back," I say, leaving her and the baby in the room.

"I need a dose of amoxicillin and Motrin for the Preston boy."

"Yes, Dr. Ashford." I fill out the necessary script for his prescription when my nurse returns with a dropper of amoxicillin and one from the Motrin. I take them back to the room and find Josie cradling her son. My heart breaks for her and her boy.

I administer his meds, not something I usually do, but I'm not done spending time with her. I'm curious what happened between her and Liam, but am not willing to entertain the idea that he's sitting at home, drinking beer, while she takes care of their son.

"He should feel better in about a half hour." I rip his prescription from my script pad and hand it to her. "Fill this and make sure you finish

the amoxicillin. He has an ear infection, but it will clear it up. You only need to give him the Motrin for today, or if he has a fever."

"Thank you."

"You're welcome, Josie. Just call if you need anything." I nod and leave the room, normal doctor procedure.

I watch as she walks out of the office. My nurse comes up behind me and clears her throat.

"Young single mom like that sure could use a nice respectable man to help take care of that baby."

"Single?" I ask, making sure my ears heard her correctly.

"Very single," she says as she pats me on my shoulder.

"Honestly, I'm not sure. I'm in love with the idea that she represented. She has a son that I raised for six years and to wake up and for them not to be there is painful. I miss him a lot. I miss being his dad and his friend, but I can't be there for him right now."

"What happened?"

I take the swing next her and move myself back and forth. "Her ex came back and it was like I didn't exist. I couldn't fight for her because she was so lost to him that I didn't stand a chance. I tried, she tried, but it was just a matter of time before she went back to him and I couldn't be there to watch that."

Chapter 3

Tonight I plan to kiss Aubrey. We've fallen into a routine; well as much as we can have here. Each night after dinner, we take a walk. Things have been platonic and I know that's because of me. Her subtle touches are telling me everything I need to know. I'm just afraid to take that step. We won't always be here and I only volunteered for one year. She lives here and plans to go to college. What if we start something only to have to end it too soon? Or what if it doesn't work out between us? I'm not sure I want the awkwardness. I can't live in fear, though.

When I walk into the clinic, Aubrey is helping an expectant mom. She looks at me with worried eyes and I know we'll be in for a long day. She settles the mom in a room and comes back with her chart.

"What's her status?" I'm in doctor mode even though she's been on my mind all day. I thought I'd get tired of seeing her, but it's been weeks since our first dinner and I've welcomed the thought of seeing her every day, whether it's at work or after.

"She'll be ready in about an hour."

"You think so?" I ask, looking up from the file.

"Yes, I'm betting dinner."

I extend my hand out to shake hers. "You're on. I'm off to see our patient."

It doesn't take long for me to assess the soon-to-be mom. She's young. She just turned fifteen. This is the part of the job I hate. I don't mind taking care of sick babies and children, but when a young girl walks in with a protruding belly, anger boils inside of me. Most of these young girls are raped when they're out in the field, working for their families. On the rare occasion one will come in with her equally young husband and I can't help but think about Noah in a few years and wonder if this could be him some day. I hope not.

I watch the clock and smile when active labor starts. Aubrey now owes me dinner. It's been an hour and a half. I walk out to get her and tap my watch. She rolls her eyes and follows me back to the room.

Aubrey administers meds, but only enough to dull the pain. I need the girl awake and functioning enough to push her baby out. We are limited here with supplies and staff so the mother needs to do more than one would be required in a modern hospital. Aubrey holds her hand, something the baby's dad or even this young girl's parents should be doing, but not in this society.

Aubrey tells her to push, but is met with resistance. This is when an additional set of hands would be helpful. Aubrey works to calm her while I carefully push the baby forward by adding pressure to her abdomen. She screams out in pain and it makes me want to kill the man that did this to her. For every beautiful thing this country offers, there is equally something disgusting to tarnish my opinion.

A local mid-wife comes in, unexpected, but definitely needed. She takes over for me so I can take care of the patient and she'll take care of the delivery. Aubrey strokes the young woman's head, whispering to her. I don't know what she's telling her, but it seems to be working. She keeps her eyes locked on Aubrey the whole time, the two of them sharing something I'll never understand and I'm okay with that. The mid-wife speaks to her and she listens. The pushing starts and within minutes the room is filled with the sweet sounds of a newborn.

I take the baby from the mid-wife and start running the standard newborn tests, making sure this precious baby is perfect. For the most part, the baby looks healthy. I wash the little girl and hand her back to her mom. The bond is instant. Regardless of how this baby was conceived, she's going to love her daughter.

I'm exhausted when I enter the makeshift bathroom. I wash my hands and splash cold water on my face. The delivery took longer than expected. When I came here I didn't know I'd be delivering babies, but I really couldn't say no. I'm here to give my services to these people who need it.

Aubrey enters. I can tell it's her. My body is already reacting to her presence. Her hands find my back and they start massaging my shoulders. I close my eyes and stay still, allowing her to work some magic on my tight muscles. Her hands feel so good, her fingers working the stiff knots. I drop to my knees so she's not reaching over me. She chuckles lightly, but moves behind me to finish the job. I roll my head from side to side as her fingers move into my hair.

I can feel her breath on my neck. Her nose skimming along my jaw, she's no longer massaging my neck. Her lips press against my neck. This isn't how I wanted our first kiss to happen. Not at work, not after an intense delivery.

I turn on my knees and face her. Her white blond hair is pulled back in a messy bun, a few loose strands framing her face. Her eyes glisten. I move the stray hair away from her face and cup her cheeks. I lean forward, kissing her lightly. I do it again with a bit more pressure. She gasps when my tongue runs along her lower lip.

She grabs a fist full of my shirt and pulls me closer, which is my signal to stop.

"We need to stop."

Her face falls and she releases my shirt. She moves back. "Oh, okay. I just thought—"

I stand and pull her hand into mine. "No, you thought right. I just don't think this is the place for us to... you know."

"Okay."

I pull her close, wrapping my arm around her waist. "Believe me when I say I want to kiss you and can't wait to collect after dinner." I kiss the top of her nose and walk out of the bathroom. I need to get away from her before lust takes over and I do something in that small room that I'll regret.

After work, I head back to the dorms. I need some time alone to think. Kissing Aubrey wasn't a mistake, but throughout the day I started questioning myself. Am I ready for a relationship?

What Josie and I had was real, at least for me, and I'm not sure I'll be able to cope with another letdown. I can't do causal. It's not in my nature, so that's out of the question. I suppose Aubrey and I need to sit down and discuss what we each want and make a decision from there. I can't get hurt again. I just can't.

I meet Aubrey out in front of the dorms once the sun goes down. They keep us fairly segregated here, with men on one side of the dorm and women on the other. Only married couples are allowed to share a room. They don't encourage fraternization either, something we need to be cautious of. I know that I don't want to get kicked out of the program.

As soon as she's out the door, I start walking toward the playground. This has been our date location since the first night. I know Aubrey owes me dinner, but we have more important things to discuss tonight.

We sit in our respective swings, swaying back and forth. The air between us is thick and that is exactly why I didn't want to kiss her at work today. I don't want there to be any awkwardness between us and now there is.

"Josie—that's my ex—I asked her to marry me something obnoxious like six times. Each time she'd say no until the last time I proposed. The only reason she said yes was because our friend had just died in a car accident. I was in the hospital when he was brought in. I was called into the emergency room to see a little girl who was having trouble breathing. When I finished with her, I saw Josie's best friend in the waiting room. I held her until they let her go in and say goodbye to her husband and then I drove her home.

"When I got home, Josie wasn't there, but our son—her son—he was asleep so I couldn't understand why she wasn't home. And then I realized that she would've gone to Katelyn's to take care of their twins. Mason and Katelyn have the cutest girls. I've been their doctor since they were born. I waited until Josie came home, sitting in the dark living room, watching as car after car shone lights into the window.

"She walked in, her tear-streaked face showing me just how desperate she was for affection. She'd just lost her best friend and didn't get to say goodbye. I held her all night. We cried together and talked about ways we needed to help Katelyn.

"When the sun rose hours later, I got down on my knee, with tears in both of our eyes and told her that I couldn't live like this anymore, that I wanted to call her my wife. I told that life was too short not to make decisions. I asked her again and for the first time in six years she didn't hesitate.

"The only problem with my proposal was that we couldn't celebrate. We couldn't tell anyone that we were finally getting married because our happiness didn't even compare to the pain we were feeling with losing Mason.

"Funeral preparations had to take place. Lives had to change. We needed to go through our daily and weekly routines minus one person. Nothing was right."

I get up and lean against the post so I can see her. "When Mason died I knew things were going to be different, but I didn't expect for my soon-to-be wife to fall out of love with me so quickly. Her ex rolled in like he hadn't been gone for ten years. I stupidly thought that she'd remember the pain he'd caused her and she'd stay far away, but they have a son and he wanted to be a part of their son's life. Not that I could blame him; Noah's an amazing kid. But that left me on the outside. As much as Josie reassured me that everything was okay, it wasn't. It didn't take long before my feelings didn't matter. And the sad thing is, I knew it was going to happen so I should've prepared myself. But I didn't. I held out hope."

I sigh and stuff my hands in my pockets. "The reason I'm telling you this is because sometimes I feel broken, like I've lost my path. The night before I left, I told her we were moving out here and she refused to come with me. I knew she was going to, but it was my last-ditch attempt. I left that night and never said goodbye to Noah, and for that I regret my decision to leave the way I did. I live with that now and am struggling to find a way to make amends. I owe it to him and myself. He needs to know that he didn't do anything wrong and that it was okay for him to choose his dad. But

I'm also telling you this because I'm looking for the whole package. I want a wife and a family sooner rather than later and I know you have your whole life ahead of you and probably don't want kids for a while, but it wouldn't be fair to either of us to start a relationship when we have different goals in life."

Aubrey stands and I prepare myself to watch her walk away. She surprises me when she steps closer, her expression unreadable in the dark. I tense when I feel her hands on my waist, fisting the sides of my shirt.

"Why don't you ask me what I want instead of assuming?"

Touché. I look down at her and smile. "What do you want, Aubrey?"

"You," she whispers.

I shake my head. Didn't she hear a single thing I just said? "I don't do casual."

"Me neither. I was raised with traditional values. When I kissed you back there it was out of emotion from what I just witnessed. When she didn't want to push, I thought for sure we were going to lose the baby. I watched you in there today. You were so calm and self-assured. I was so impressed with how you handled everything. I couldn't help myself when I found you hunched over the sink. I needed to touch you. I needed the peace I feel when you're near me."

I take a deep breath. I'm not trying to push her away. I'm just not looking for anything temporary. "I'm leaving soon. I'm only here for a year."

"I'm a volunteer with my parent's missionary, Nick. I can come and go as I please. I don't have to put in a year or even a month. If I want to go to another hospital tomorrow, I can."

I run my hand through my hair. She makes everything so tempting, but I don't know if that's enough. "What are you saying?"

She steps closer, her chest pressing against mine. I wish it was light enough so I can see her face. See her expression. Her lips graze just below my chin. I can't help but smile; she can't reach me unless I bend over.

Aubrey wraps her arms around me, resting her head on my chest. I do the same, resting my head on top of hers, and look out into the darkness. I wish life could be simple.

"When I first started here I wasn't sure I was going to stay. I had told my parents that I wanted to explore each village and find the best one for me. My mom expected me to return to South Africa and go to college for fashion design or something stupid like that. She was always saying I'd decorate before I healed. I had to prove her wrong.

"The morning you walked in, I forgot to breathe. I choked on my own tongue. It's not because you're gorgeous and strikingly handsome, which in case you have any doubt, you absolutely are; it's because of the way you carried yourself. You walked in like you were the leader and there to make a change. I was this new nurse and watched the others fawn all over you and you didn't even recognize the attention you were getting.

"I thought 'wow, his wife is one lucky woman' only to find out that you weren't married. My hopes soared, but you wouldn't talk to me. You were—still are—water cooler talk. The nurses, they adore you, and here I am in your arms, trying to find a way to keep you. I don't know if I believe in fate or fairytales, but the moment you walked into the clinic on my first day, I knew I was in trouble.

"I want to try, if you do. You make all the ugly in this world seem just a bit better when I close my eyes at night and I'd be a fool to let you walk away because you don't do casual."

I take in her words. They hit me square in the heart. But there is one question I need to know. I lean down and whisper, "Would you come back to the States with me?" I feel her reaction before she says the words. She starts nodding.

"We were destined to meet, Nick. I have no doubt in my mind you were meant for me. If you want me to move back to the States with you, I'd gladly walk by your side into your next adventure."

I don't wait another minute. I capture her lips with mine. In my heart, I know she's speaking the truth. I can feel it. The loss is immediate when she pulls away.

"Where are you going?"

She holds my hands, extending our arms out wide. "Have you ever done anything spontaneous?"

I try to pull her back to me. This is the only time we can touch and she's just declared that she'll follow me anywhere and now she's standing too far away.

I shrug. I can't remember the last time I was spontaneous, aside from asking Josie to marry me.

"Can't say that I have," I reply. I finally give up and drag her back toward the dorm. I can't see her face and it's driving me nuts. I stop us just outside of our residence. There is enough light that we can see each other when we talk. I like this better, although we'll have to keep our voices down. "Now tell me what's going on in that mind of yours."

Her grin is wicked with an evil little glint in her eyes. She's up to something and I have a feeling I'm going to be on the receiving end whether I like it or not. I pull her to me, my hand cupping the back of her head, holding her to me as I kiss her deeply. The man in me wants to take her. Make her mine. The volunteer in me knows we have to abide by the rules. They are set that way to protect us. As much as I want to say screw it and take her back to my room, I know I can't.

"Marry me?"

Chapter 4

"Why not, Josie? We live together. We are raising your son as our own. We celebrate holidays and birthdays as a family. Tell me why not after three years? Why don't you want to marry me?"

Josie looks at me with tears in her eyes. She wipes them angrily, smearing her make-up in the process. "I don't know."

"That's not a reason and you know it." I kick my shoes off and head to her bedroom. I'm done calling it our bedroom. Clearly I'm in the wrong here, thinking we have something special.

I stare into the closet and look at my clothes next to hers. I can't stay here, not tonight. Not after this second rejection. My suitcase mocks me in the corner, reminding me that nothing in this house, aside from clothes and a few books, is mine. I moved into her home. I never gave it a second thought. Noah's stuff is here and it made sense. The house is big enough for the three of us, even though I want to expand our family.

I think I need to give her space. Maybe that's the only answer. I pull my suitcase out of the closet and set it on the bed. The zipper is loud, echoing throughout the room. I shake my head as I start unloading my side of the dresser. The anger builds with each load until I'm throwing stuff into the dark hole.

Yanking my shirts and slacks off the hangers, they go flying, hitting the walls and ceiling. I know I'm making more noise than necessary, but I'm pissed. Why does she keep saying no and when am I going to grow a fucking set and just leave her? Clearly she doesn't love me like I love her. I'm always battling a ghost for her affection.

"What are you doing?"

I look at her, standing in the doorway of the closet, my breathing labored. "What does it look like I'm doing?"

"It looks like you're leaving me."

"Ding… ding… ding... Johnny, tell her what she's won." I step to her. "Well, Johnny, Ms. Preston has won her life back. She no longer has to pretend to be in love with the good doctor." I turn away before I can see her reaction. I may have been a little harsh, but I don't care. I'm done being the only one to put effort into our relationship. I stalk past her, bumping her shoulder as I pass.

"You can't do this."

"Yes I can." I throw my pile of clothes into my suitcase and head to the bathroom. She steps in front of me, blocking my path. If I didn't love her, I'd pick her up and move her out of my way. I tower over her. She's my little rag doll. "Move, Josephine."

"You can't leave me."

"Unbelievable. You want me to stay? You want me to live here knowing that you don't love me? The first time I understood; we hadn't been together that long. But now? There's no excuse. You don't love me, I get that. I'll get my things and be out of your hair in an hour."

Josie puts her hands on my chest, stopping me from moving. "I do love you, Nick. I love you so much, but I'm scared. I'm so scared that I'm going to say yes and everything will change. I love the life we share and marriage changes things. It changes people."

"I want a life with you, Josie. I want to have a baby."

She looks away and I know in my heart that she's not ready for that. Being a mom at eighteen really does a number on some people.

"I'm not ready."

"Yeah, I know. But I am and I need to think about me, too. Three years, Josie. Most women are begging their men to ask them after one. I've asked twice and each time you've turned me down. I can't take any more rejection."

"Nick, I love you. I do. I'm scared." Her hands move up my chest. I know I should stop her advances, but I can't. I'm putty when it comes to her. I've wanted her for so long I'm willing to torture myself just to keep her.

"I'm scared I'm going to lose you."

"You won't lose me," she says as her fingers unbutton my shirt. I need to tell her no. We've been down this path before. It leads to the bed, amazing sex and me forgetting how we got to this point.

My hands clamp down on her wrist, stopping her from finishing the job. "It won't work this time."

I move aside and leave her standing in her room. I don't know where I'm going, but I need to get out of this house and away from her. She's an evil temptress who knows how to get her way with me and I need to think clearly.

I drive to Ralph's. It's dead, which is surprising. I pull up a stool at the bar and signal for a beer. The stool next to me moves and I can feel the person next to me sigh.

"That didn't take long."

"They're women, they talk." Mason says and he takes a sip of his beer.

"I give up, man. I can't do it anymore."

"I hear ya."

I look at him out of the corner of my eye. "Aren't you supposed to convince me to go back to her?"

He shakes his head and starts peeling the label off his bottle. "Nope, I told Katelyn I won't do that. Josie doesn't make sense. Her world revolves around you and Noah and yet she isn't willing to make it official. I'm not even going to pretend to understand what she's thinking."

"She's scared things are going to change."

"They will, but it's nothing to be scared about. Hell, I just about pissed myself before I asked Katelyn to marry me."

I chuckle. "You've been doing that since high school."

"Nah man, not like that. The moment I decided I was asking her and went to ask her parents, I threw up in their bushes. I was a nervous wreck, afraid they wouldn't think I was good enough for their daughter. And the day I asked, I think I pissed myself a little when she said yes. If you ever tell her that, though, I'll deny it and you'll never be allowed at my house."

I can't help but laugh. I have no doubt Mason is telling the truth.

"Mr. Preston has given me his blessing. It was easy to ask him. I think he was expecting it."

"I'm sure he was. He likes you."

"Josie doesn't."

Mason asks for two more beers and a bowl of peanuts. He's always eating, but I can't help but grab a few.

"Josie loves you and I know you love her. I think that sometimes you just have to wait shit out if you really want to be with that person. I know she's a pain in the ass, but she's worth it."

"I'm not sure if she loves me or the idea of me. I think she's afraid of being alone."

Mason whacks me on the back of my head. I give him the 'what the fuck' look and he just smiles. "If I didn't think she loves you, I wouldn't be sitting here when I have a hot little thing waiting for me at home. Believe me, Ashford, you may be taller and pretty, but you don't have jack shit on Katelyn."

"Does she know you talk about her like that?"

"Yep, and she loves it."

Again, I have no doubt he's telling the truth. It takes someone special to love someone like Mason.

"What should I do?"

"Go home and make love to her and be patient. She went through more than anyone should ever have to go through and she's scared. Accept it and either move on or forget about her reasons and just be with her. I guarantee she's not going anywhere. I see the way she looks at you. You've made her feel whole again. If you leave her because she's scared it makes you no better than the other guy."

"The other guy was your best friend."

Mason downs the rest of his beer and throws some cash on the bar. "Yeah, well he's not anymore."

I watch as he leaves, replaying everything that he said. He's right in his own way. Love should be more important than anything else and I love her. I love her more than anything in my life aside from Noah. I can still be his dad without sharing his last name.

When I get home, the house is dark. I open the door to find her sitting in one of our kitchen chairs, in the entryway. She's making it so I don't miss her. She looks up at me with her red, puffy face and it breaks my heart. I shut the door quietly and lean against it. I'm not sure I'm ready to talk about what happened earlier.

"You can't leave me."

"I know." I drop down on my knees and bury my face in her lap. Mason's right. I love her too much to leave her. We can work through this, figure out a compromise. I'll do anything I can to keep her.

"I love you so much, Nick. I can't lose you."

"You won't, baby. I'm not going anywhere."

"I'll give you a baby if that's what you want."

I look at her, shocked at what she just said. I shake my head. "As much as I want to have a baby with you, we can wait until you're ready."

She pulls me close. Locking her arms around my neck, I pick her up and carry her to our bedroom. I look around and notice the room is clean. She's put away my clothes and made it look like nothing bad happened in here.

I lay her down gently, pulling off her shirt. She removes her shorts as I stand and strip bare for her...

Chapter 5

"Knock, knock," I look up from my desk to find my co-worker, Roman, standing in the doorway.

"Come in," I say, clearing my voice. I can't believe I remembered that fight with Josie. I thought for sure I was leaving her then, but no, like the idiot I am, I stayed and took more of her punishment.

"Are you all packed?"

I look around the sparse room. Only my roommate hung pictures. I brought my clothes and one picture of Noah. That was the extent of my personal possessions.

"Yeah, just had my clothes. I didn't bring much with me."

"It's a shame you aren't staying longer. We could really use you around here."

I smile and nod in thanks. "It's time for me to head back home. I have a practice there that I really need to get back to. I told my sub I'd be gone a year and I miss my patients."

"I understand," he says. He taps me on my shoulder. "I'll see you downstairs in a few minutes."

I turn back to my desk and finish what I was working on. It's hard to believe that my year is up. I've learned so much and can't wait to get back home to Beaumont and join my practice again. I know that when I see Josie, I'll be able to smile at her and wish her a good day. I no longer harbor those types of feelings for her. I finish the letter I'm leaving for my replacement and set down my pen.

With one last look I walk into the great room. My friends are all here to say goodbye. I seek out Aubrey as she extends her hand to mine, linking our fingers together. We've been together for three months now. I know it's not a long time by some standards, but for us it's enough. Tonight, when we reach London, I'll finally be able to make love to her. We've waited. We've been good. And until last night we hid our relationship from our colleagues. We know some suspected, but we kept everything platonic and professional during the daylight hours.

When Aubrey asked me to marry her, I wanted to say no, but then I remembered what it felt like each time Josie said that word and I couldn't do that to her. Unconventional? Yes, but perfect for us.

We walk hand in hand to the center of the room where the pastor is set up. I kiss her hand and look at him, nodding that we're ready.

"We're gathered here to celebrate the union of Nicholas and Aubrey…" I look at her, giddy with excitement. She's going to be my wife and she's coming back to Beaumont with me. She's hasn't decided what she wants to do. I told her I didn't care. As long as she was with me, it didn't matter. Secretly, I'm hoping there's a baby in our future and that she'll want to stay home and be a mom. But if not, so be it. We'll be together. That's all that matters.

When I look at her, I know what true love feels like. It's the butterflies you get every time that person walks into the room or you get a whiff of their perfume from another room. Aubrey does that to me. I knew that night, not so long ago, when I opened up to her, that she'd be my wife. If I had to stay here another year to prove it, I would've, but I'm thankful she was smart enough for the both of us.

I soon realize I was too focused on watching her that I missed my ceremony. "You may kiss your bride," the pastor says. I pull her close, my hands cupping her delicate face and press my lips to hers.

"I now give you, Dr. and Mrs. Ashford."

We raise our hands to the cheering of our friends. We walk down the aisle hand in hand. I pick up our bags and we head to the waiting van. Aubrey gives out hugs while I load our bags. I stand there watching her and thank God every day for her. She showed me the true meaning of love and patience. Maybe I should thank Liam. If he hadn't shown up, I probably wouldn't be here today.

I lift my bride into the van and wave at everyone as we head off into the sun to start our next chapter.

Chapter 6

"Good morning." My lips skim against her bare skin, desperate for her. Since arriving in Beaumont our honeymoon has come to a screeching halt. I suppose living with your new in-laws, ones you've never met, sort of kills the mood. I've promised her we'd move as soon as we found a place of our own.

"What's so good about it?" I pull her blanket down slightly, uncovering more of her. For two weeks I've grown accustomed to her sleeping in the nude and now she's covered in a very offensive tank top. I kiss my way down her body, lifting the hem of her shirt, placing my lips on her back.

"Nick." She mumbles into her pillow. One thing I learned about Aubrey since being here is that she does not like the cold. At all. Not even in the cute winter jacket my mom picked up for her. I suppose I should've warned her before we got married, but honestly the thought never crossed my mind.

I flip her over and attack her lips. This is as far as we can go and it sucks. Falling in love with her in Africa was hard enough, but to have already had her and not be able to touch her is going to be the death of me.

"What do you want to do today?" I trail my lips over her collarbone.

"Don't you have to work?"

"Doctors don't work on the weekends."

Aubrey adjusts under my weight, causing more problems. I groan and bury my face in her neck.

"I want to look for an apartment or a house. Something for us to live in as husband and wife because I'm getting really needy."

I sigh. "I know, me too." I rise up and look at my wife. I can't believe that just over a year ago I was arriving in Africa with my tail between my legs and my heart broken. I knew I'd return home, but I didn't bank on a wife coming back with me. "I love you."

"I love you too." She pulls me close and kisses me deeply, making me pull away all too soon.

"House hunting it is." I jump up and get out of bed with my mind set on a cold shower.

"I want to go to that little café on Main Street for lunch. Can we do that?"

It's a good thing my back is turned because the expression on my face will tell her exactly what my brain is saying. Hell no.

"Sure, babe." I exit the room as quickly as I can.

I love our Sunday afternoons. Noah goes to the Preston's and we get to just relax. Today, Josie has a surprise for me. I've tried to figure it out, but she's kept it a secret. Even Katelyn wouldn't tell me.

Josie drives us to the park. I look at her questioningly; she just shrugs playfully as she gets out of the car. I follow and jog to catch up with her. I reach for her hand, bringing it to my lips. I place a lingering kiss and wish my ring were gracing her finger.

I can't help but think this is the right moment. The one I've been waiting for. But I can't take any more rejection. I've resigned myself to living as her partner and not her husband. It's not going to be enough, but I'll find a way to make it work.

Josie leads us to the park bench that faces Main Street. About two years ago the city officials decided to revitalize this area. Wrought iron light poles were installed, a nice fence put up around the park and park benches were added. Across from the park, businesses started rebuilding and redoing their façades, bringing back the old hometown feel. The only problem with it is some couldn't afford to upgrade and their businesses folded, leaving empty storefronts.

We sit down, her hand in my lap. I love this. I love that we are a couple, raising our son and living a fulfilling life. I don't need her to have my last name to make us a family. We already are.

"What are we doing here?" I look around and wonder why of all the benches she chose, we're on the one facing the dilapidated building.

"What do you see when you look at that building?"

"Ruins."

"No, Nick. Really look at it. What do you see?"

I do as she asks and study the building. It was once a toy store. Mr. Preston told me that he worked there when he was a youngster and that he learned to carve a wooden train from the owner, Mr. W. He said no one knew what the W stood for and no one ever bothered to ask. He died a few years back and didn't have a family to run the store for him. It had been empty and falling apart since.

"I see the toy store in its heyday. Kids running to the shop after school to see what new toys Mr. W made."

"My dad would've done that."

"I know that's how I can picture it. He tells Noah about what it was like all the time. Tell me, Josie, what do you see?"

Her expression is what I want to see when I ask her to marry me. Her face lights up, her eyes go wide and her grin is from ear to ear. It breaks my heart to know that an empty, broken-down store can get the reaction that I so desperately need.

"I see my dream."

"Your dream?" I don't mean to sound like an insensitive boyfriend, but this is the first time I'd heard of a dream.

"I want to open a flower shop in the old toy store and call it Whimsicality."

"Why?"

Josie looks at me and I can't decipher if she's pissed off or genuinely concerned that I don't know the answer to my own question.

"I want to bring the same happiness Mr. W. did to people, but with flowers."

"Okay."

"I talked to my dad. He'll give me the loan to get started and Henry is going to do all the construction at cost."

I see the way she talks about her dream and know that she'll be successful. I can see everything taking shape in her mind and in mine. The sheer joy that is showing on her face as she talks about opening a shop is mesmerizing. If this is what she wants to do, we'll make it happen.

"When do we get started?"

Josie jumps into my lap and wraps her arms tight around my neck. I start to think this could be the moment, but hold back and just enjoy what we are celebrating.

"Nick, are you coming?"

I blink a few times to clear my thoughts. I don't know what I expected. Maybe I thought the park bench would be gone, or this café never took off. I'm wrong on both accounts. Aubrey has to drag me down the street since my feet decide they no longer function for their intended purposes.

I think about telling her that I don't feel well and that I need to rest before returning to work tomorrow, but I owe her this. I can't expect her to stay cooped up in my parent's house the whole time. I want Beaumont to be her home and sadly that means I'll be running into Josie.

"I've been dying to try this café since your mom and I drove by it the other day." Aubrey climbs the three steps that lead to the café. When Josie told me about the expansion I flipped. I thought she only wanted to do it so Liam had a place to play. I told her it was stupid and a waste of money. Looks like I was wrong.

There are only a few chairs available with a line of people at the counter. No music right now, thank God. I don't know what I'd do if I saw Liam. I know we are going to end up talking sooner or later, but I'm hoping for much later. Actually what I'm hoping for is to find out he's gone back to L.A., leaving Josie here. At least then I can be in Noah's life and have a somewhat reasonable relationship with him.

I stand in line behind Aubrey. Josie has created one large space, combining the flower shop and the coffee shop into one. I look around for Jenna, but don't find her. I always liked her. She was real good to Josie when we were dating.

"Why are you so fidgety?"

"I'm not."

"Yes, you are. Here, give me a kiss." Aubrey pulls me down, not afraid of public displays of affection. I pull away from her when

I hear a throat clearing. I look up and instantly wish I was back in Africa.

I wish I had a mirror so I could see what my face looks like because Josie's face is impassive. I look at Aubrey, who is oblivious to what is going on and back at Josie, who smiles softly as if she's simply greeting the next customer.

Aubrey steps forward and places her order. Josie is calm, respectful, but I can see the questions swirling in her mind. I know what she's thinking and for some reason it bothers me. Why is it okay for her to move on, but I can't? I see the ring on her finger, the one I so fiercely tried to cover. I notice her eyes as they travel down my hand and then over to Aubrey's. We wear simple wedding bands, nothing flashy or eye-popping, but enough for us and the moment when we said our vows. She doesn't show any sign of recognition. No annoyance or happiness.

"What can I get for you, Nick?" I thought that hearing her voice for the first time in over a year would bring back the pain I felt when I left, but it doesn't. My heart isn't aching and threatening to burst out of my chest. I'm not remembering the night I left or the life I left behind. The shared kisses and romantic moments that we had aren't flooding my conscious. I look down at my wife and know that I've married my soul mate. I kiss her on the nose, thankful that I made the decision—the right one for me—and married her. "Just black, Josie."

The recollection of our long, heart-felt conversations is evident on Aubrey's face. I'm not sure what to expect. We didn't talk about my life back here and what it would mean when we came face to face with my past.

Aubrey turns and extends her hand to Josie. I watch as my former love and my forever love shake hands. "It's nice to meet you. I've heard so much about you."

Josie's face deadpans and as much as I want to laugh, I know she's thinking the most horrible things. "I'm sure you have." Josie glances away and busies herself with our order.

"Nick wouldn't say anything bad about you. He has the utmost respect for you."

Josie dips her head slightly. I know she's having a hard time believing Aubrey. I probably have every right to sling her name, but I didn't and I won't. We are adults and things happen. Am I upset? Yes, but not because we aren't together...because I've lost Noah.

"I'll bring over your coffee," she says as she disappears behind the large coffee machine.

I guide Aubrey to a table and pull out her chair. When I sit, I inspect the café. Needless to say, I'm shocked. When Josie bought this run-down space I never expected we'd be able to make her dream come true. Only days after opening *Whimsicality* she had a line out the door and down the street, all just to buy flowers. The four of us—Mason, Katelyn, Josie and I—worked night and day to get the place up and running. I took a week off, our planned vacation to Disney World canceled, to help open the store. I should've been more accepting when she came home with her expansion plans, but we all knew how I felt about those.

I'm happy for her. I'm happy for me.

"Are you going to ask her?" Aubrey snaps me out of my musing.

"Ask her what?"

“If you can see Noah.”

“No.” I pull out a packet of sugar and fiddle with it.

Aubrey places her hand gently on mine. I move mine ever so slightly so I can hold her hand. “Noah is the one person you talked about daily. You need this, Nick. You need to see him and tell him that you’re sorry for leaving.”

“I don’t know. She has no reason to let me see him.”

“Just ask.”

I don’t respond because Josie is making her way toward us. She sets down our coffee and an assortment of pasties.

“On the house.” She plasters on a smile and I can’t tell if it’s fake or not.

Aubrey kicks my leg. I scowl at her, but the look she’s giving me is much worse. I have a feeling if I don’t do as she suggests, I’m in for it.

I look at Josie, who is observing the both of us. I can’t maintain eye contact with her. I don’t know what I’ll do if I see the negative look in her eyes when I ask.

“Can I see Noah?”

Chapter 7

I want to take back the words as soon as I say them. I should've waited. Asking her today, the first day that she knows I'm back in town, is probably not the best idea. I'm afraid to look at her for fear that the answer is written all over her face. I'm not sure I can handle this rejection. I need to see him, apologize for my actions, and ask for his forgiveness. He's by far the most important person in my life, aside from Aubrey, and I want to have any semblance of a relationship I can with him. I think I'm at least owed that.

Josie takes a step back. My eyes are on her now, waiting for her reaction. She looks around the shop, smiling at the patrons who have just walked in. She hangs her head. Is she ashamed?

"This isn't a conversation for here, Nick."

"Where can this conversation take place?"

"I don't know. I wasn't expecting to see you."

"Yeah, well I wasn't expecting a lot of things, but life has a funny way of determining its own path." I try to hide the sarcasm in my voice. Deep down, I know she had no choice when it came to Liam. I just wanted to hope that I was enough for her.

"Where are you staying?"

I want to shout 'in the house we shared' but I bite my tongue. That was always her house. I just squatted in it for years.

"We've been staying at my parents, but we just rented a loft across from the park."

Josie looks out the window. I know she can see the loft from here. This is what Aubrey wants and I'm not going to deny her.

"When are you moving in?"

"We'll be in by next weekend."

Josie nods. "What if Liam and I come over to your place? We'll bring dinner and we can all sit down and talk about what's best for Noah."

I look to Aubrey, who nods. I'll never thank her enough for being supportive of me having a relationship with another woman's son.

"My number hasn't changed," I say. "Why don't you hash out the details with Liam and call me."

"Okay." Josie leaves and tends to her other customers. In the past, I'd watch her walk away. Let my eyes linger on her body longer than necessary. But not now. With one last glance at her retreating form, I shake my head. Aubrey's thumb caresses over the top of my hand.

"You did well."

"I feel like an idiot. I'm setting myself up."

"Why do you say that?"

"Liam and I are anything but friends. He has no reason to let me see his son."

Aubrey leans over the table. I meet her half way and kiss her lightly. "Everyone is reasonable. You just have to believe."

I want to tell her she's wrong, that not everyone is reasonable, especially Liam Westbury or Page, whatever he goes by now. I also need to find the right moment to tell her that I hate the tank top that she sleeps in and that she's about to meet the lead singer of the band that adorns her chest at night. I didn't know she was a fan until we got here. I suppose 'who's your favorite band' was a topic of conversation we should've had in Africa. Not a conversation I'm excited to have.

We hold hands as we walk down the street. Aubrey huddles close to me, cold. I feel bad for her and know that we need to hit the mall and buy her some more functional clothes. The stuff she bought with my mother is too… fashionable. Or maybe she just needs to get used to the cold. I mean, it's not that cold, but it is when you've lived in the scorching heat your whole life. I wrap my arm around her, hoping to provide more body heat.

I pull us up short and unlock the red door that leads to my practice. When she steps inside, her eyes go wide. My practice is decorated in reds, blues and greens on one side and pinks, purples and yellows on the other. In one corner stands a dollhouse and a cradle filled with baby dolls and a plastic play family. The boy's side has fire trucks, building blocks and army figures that Noah insisted on putting in here.

Aubrey steps away from me and looks around. "You made your office a fun zone."

I come up behind her, encasing her in my arms. I like that I can rest my head on top of hers. It makes me feels as if I'm protecting her somehow. "Little kids hate the doctor's office. They know this is where they come to get shots. I had to give them a little bit of happiness."

"It's great."

I rub my hands up and down her arms. "Come on, I'll show you around." I take her hand in mine and lead her down the hall. I love the reaction I get when we step into each room. This was the first thing I did when I took over this practice—repainted each room and gave it a theme. Rooms here don't have numbers; they have names. The Jungle Room, The Fire Truck Room and Noah's least favorite, the Barbie Room.

I save my office for last. Not because I'm proud of it, but because it's boring and drab. I open the door and flick on the light. The walls are bare, stark white and recently painted. When I left, I took everything down so my replacement could feel at home. I guess she removed her stuff when she left the other night.

Standing in the center of my office, I take it all in and what it means to me. This is my livelihood and I should've never left my patients, but I needed to volunteer. I needed to feel as if my life meant something. I was spiraling out of control and that was the only way to find some balance.

As much as it pained me to leave, staying wasn't the answer. I have so much to thank Africa for, mostly my wife, but also giving me the time to heal without seeing the life I had walking around with someone else. I think seeing them together, as a family, would've done me in.

"What are you thinking about?" Aubrey steps in front of me, making herself the focal point of my attention.

I push her hair off her shoulder and nuzzle her cheek. "Thank you my sweet, beautiful and sexy wife."

"For what?" She giggles lightly, my scruff tickling her.

I pull back and look at her. I let my hand linger on the back of her head, my fingers tangling in her hair. "For being understanding. For not overreacting when you met Josie and for encouraging me to ask about Noah even though I was scared."

"I know how much he means to you. I may not be a mother, but if my ex raised my child I would have thought that I'd have enough love in my heart to let him be a part of their life."

The simple mention of a child stirs my insides. I didn't know men had a biological clock and if this is how women feel, I finally understand the pressure. I want to have a baby with her, but don't want to pressure her. I'm hoping now that we are here and we're settling down, she'll want to make us parents.

I can picture her so clearly with a rounded belly, sitting in the park, reading a book. Everything about her would be perfect. I'd count the hours until I could be home with her. I'd want to touch her constantly, to feel what it feels when the baby kicks. To talk, sing, read and tell stories to our baby. I want to see her like this. I want us to have this happiness.

"Where'd you go just now?"

She knows me so well.

"I was thinking about us having a baby," I say.

"Oh yeah?"

I nod. "Yeah."

"Do you think you maybe want to try?"

I can't help but smile. "There's no maybes, Aubrey. I want to try."

"You don't want to wait until we've been married longer?" Aubrey unzips my coat and pushes it off my shoulder. I have no choice but to let go of her so it can fall to the ground. She pulls my tucked-in shirt out of my jeans and her cold hands make me shiver.

"What are you doing, Aubs?"

She steps back and gazes into my eyes. First her scarf and then her coat come off. It's cold in here, she's going to freeze. She pulls her sweater over her head. Her turtleneck follows. Her hands reach around her back. I watch as her bra straps become loose on her shoulders, as they slide down her arms and finally fall to the floor onto the mound of clothing that is collecting there. I shed my sweater and unbutton my shirt, sliding it off. We are both standing in the middle of my office, naked from the chest up.

Aubrey steps closer, her fingers reaching out and tracing the muscular ridges in my chest. "I thought maybe my husband would want to try and have a baby."

"In here?" My voice cracks like a teenager.

She looks around with a wicked gleam on her face. "Hell yeah, in here. I have a hot doctor for a husband. I think it's about time we christened his desk." She rubs her hand down the front of my jeans, adding pressure to my bulge. "And maybe his chair after that," she says as she bites down on my nipple.

My eyes roll back in my head as her mouth assaults my chest and her hand works me out of my jeans. My fingers deftly unbutton her jeans and get the zipper down so I can push them over her hips. She wiggles, helping them move down her legs. I touch her where I want her most and lose all inhibitions. I pick her up, her delightful squeals telling me that this is exactly what she wants, and set her down roughly on my desk.

She sends papers flying and starts laughing. "I've always wanted to do that."

"Me too," I say as my lips capture hers. I pull off her shoes and pant legs. This isn't going to be romantic or pretty. Her hands pull down my boxers, letting my dick spring free. I close my eyes when she starts stroking me.

"I need you, Nick."

I pull her forward, wrapping her legs around my waist and give in to her needs.

Chapter 8

As we unpack the final box of dishes, I set them in the dishwasher for a quick wash. Josie and Liam will be here in an hour and, as promised, they are bringing dinner. Believe me, I have my reservations about eating anything that Liam has purchased, but I'm willing to do anything to see Noah.

Our loft has two large bedrooms and one smaller. It's more space than we need right now, but Aubrey fell in love as soon as we opened the door. I can't blame her. The living room windows face the park—and while some may not like that—we definitely do.

We outfitted our new home with brand-new everything. We had to. Anything that I did keep from when I moved in with Josie is outdated and honestly, not a time that I want to remember.

Aubrey comes into the kitchen, her newly acquired coconut-lime lotion wafting through the room. She brings her arms around my front, kissing my shoulder blade. This can mean only one thing—she's wearing heels. I turn in her arms and kiss her forehead, her eyes, her nose, and finally her lips. We need to have a conversation about our dinner guests. I know I should've told her sooner and by sooner I mean when we were getting to know each other. But seriously, how do you say 'hey my ex dumped me for her ex who just happens to be Liam Page'? It's really an ego issue and I didn't need mine to be deflated any more than it already was.

"I need to tell you something important." My words are soft. I push her hair off her shoulder and cup her face, my thumb caressing her soft cheek. I love how soft her skin is.

"Am I going to be upset?"

I shrug. I really don't know, but I hope not. "It's about Josie and Liam."

"Okay," she says as she steps back, but I won't have it. I put my hand on her waist and hold her to me.

"You have nothing to worry about, but you might be mad at me because I kept this from you. When I think about it now, it's silly. I should've told you, but it's not something I like to think about or even care about."

"Just tell me, Nick."

I sigh and close my eyes. What if she thinks I'm less of man? When I open my eyes she's looking at me with such concern that it breaks my heart. I shake my head and blurt out, "Liam is Liam Page of 4225 West."

Aubrey steps back and this time I let her. I don't know what she's thinking. Her eyes wander and I can tell there are a million thoughts running through her head.

"Is this why you hate my tank top?"

I try not to smile, but it's to no avail. I nod, afraid that if I say yes it will sound as if I'm jealous. I know I used to be back in high school, but I grew out of that. I'd like to think I'm more mature than to be jealous of Liam, even now. The only thing he has that I want is Noah.

"You went to high school with Liam Page?"

"Westbury, but yeah."

"How did you meet Josie?"

"High school. I had a crush, but she was with Liam. I went away to college, determined to finish in four years, and when I came back she was in my office one day with a sick toddler."

"He left her?"

"Long story, but yes he did. In his defense, he didn't know about Noah."

"And now he's coming to our house for dinner?"

I nod.

"Are you afraid I'll fall at his feet?"

"No," I say but my voice cracks when I answer. I hang my head. I hate the feeling that he has a hold over me, but hell if the thought doesn't cross my mind.

Aubrey steps closer. Her fingers splay out in my hair. "If I had known, I wouldn't wear the shirt. I'm not a fan by any means. I've heard them a few times and my friend gave the shirt to me. I'll get rid of it, but for the record, Liam Page has nothing on you!"

I capture her lips. My hands cup her ass to bring her closer. I've never been so in love and I know now that my love for Josie stemmed from a high school infatuation. I have no doubt we loved each other, but not in the way that counts at the end of the night.

With a loud knock I pull away from her lips. I kiss her once more before pulling her hand into mine. We walk to the door to greet our guests. If someone had told me a year ago that I'd be eating dinner with Liam, Josie by his side, I probably would've punched them, but here we are, about to be civil adults. At least I hope Liam is civil because he's the one who stands in my way of seeing Noah, even if it's for one last time.

I open the door wide with Aubrey standing just behind me, one hand on my bicep, the other on my back. Josie and Liam stand before us. Josie's smiling and Liam's looking down at the ground. He doesn't want to be here any more than I want him here.

"Come in," I say in a fake 'I'm so happy you're invading my space' voice. Josie grabs Liam's hand and pulls him into our place.

"Can I take your coats?"

"Sure," Josie says as Liam helps her out of her jacket. He folds it across his arm and somehow maneuvers his off without setting Josie's down. He hands them both to Aubrey, who nods graciously.

"This is nice," Josie says as she looks around. I shrug and put my hands into my pockets. Liam and I don't need to shake hands; there's no need to get reacquainted.

Aubrey returns and slides her arm into my mine. I look down at her and try to fake a smile, but I know it is more of a grimace. I need to snap out of it and be a host or this night will be ruined.

I clear my throat. "Josie you remember my wife, Aubrey. And this is Liam." I'm speechless when Liam steps forward and shakes her hand.

"It's nice to meet you, Aubrey."

"Nice to meet you, too. Thanks for coming."

"Oh here," Josie holds up a plastic bag. "We brought Chinese. I hope you like it. I know Nick and Liam do, but didn't really know what you liked, but I thought that most people like Chinese—"

"Josie," Liam interrupts her.

"What?"

"You're rambling. I'm sure Aubrey likes Chinese. Let's just eat or whatever."

Aubrey takes the bag from Josie. "Here, let me get these out of the cartons and on the table. Go ahead and make yourself comfortable. Nick, why don't you get drinks for everyone?" She gives me a kiss before she retires to the kitchen.

I watch as she retreats.

"She's very pretty, Nick."

I nod, not ready to take my eyes off the entryway leading to the kitchen. I sigh and finally look at Josie who now has Liam's arm around her waist. "She is. What can I get you to drink?"

"Whatever you have is fine."

"Liam, do you want a beer? I have these new microbrews that I picked up."

"Yeah, sure, that'd be great."

I excuse myself and almost collide with Aubrey when she comes out of the kitchen. I kiss her briefly on the cheek. I hear her talking to Josie and it makes me smile. Maybe they can be friends. Aubrey could use a friend, but I wouldn't want her to feel awkward.

I pour Aubrey and Josie each an iced tea and grab beers for Liam and me. When I get to the dining room area, they are all sitting around chatting, even Liam, which surprises me. He thanks me and twists off the top before taking a sip.

I sit next to Aubrey and we all dig in. Maybe it's best that we eat before we get down to business.

"So Aubrey, what do you do?"

Aubrey sets her fork down and holds her napkin to her mouth while she swallows her food. "Nothing yet."

Josie's eyes go wide and I know what she's thinking.

Aubrey waves her hands in the air. "Oh no, don't think anything bad. This is my first time in the U.S. Nick wanted me to get to know Beaumont before I find a job."

She looks over at me and smiles. She's right. She doesn't need to work.

"Well if you find yourself bored, I'm hiring," Josie says.

"What happened to Jenna?"

Josie looks at me. "Jenna is still there, but the shop is busy."

"Thanks for the offer, Josie," Aubrey says. "I'll consider it."

That answer seems to be enough for Josie, as she nods and continues to eat. Aubrey looks at me and her eyebrows go up, her silent way of telling me to ask the question that brings us all together. But I can't seem to find my tongue.

I shake my head and continue to eat, refusing to make eye contact with her or anyone else at the table.

Liam and I help ourselves to seconds as the ladies chat about everything from fashion to the latest movies. They seem to be getting along great and that means a lot to me. I'd like for Aubrey to have some friends here and it's not that I'd expect an invite to Katelyn's for Sunday football, but it would be nice to have my friends back.

Liam sets his fork down and clears his throat. He rests his hands on the table and folds them. I don't know what's about to happen, but I have a feeling I'm not going to like it. The Liam I know from high school wasn't reasonable and he has no reason to be now.

He's about to rip my heart out of my chest and there isn't shit I can do about it.

Chapter 9

I resign myself to accepting the worse. If I was in Liam's shoes I wouldn't want my son to have anything to do with his mother's ex. I should never have asked. I should've just waited until I saw him again and asked how he's doing, just like any other doctor would do...and try to forget the countless hours I've spent with him. After tonight, all I'm going to have is memories.

My hands clench under the table when Liam looks at me.

"When I came back, I wasn't planning on staying. I had a life away from here and, as much as I wanted to see Josie, I wasn't going to interrupt her life. But then I saw Noah and I knew there was no way I was letting him go."

Liam picks up Josie's hand and kisses it. There's no denying the love they have for each other.

"If it was up to me, you'd never see Noah again. I'm that selfish of a man when it comes to him. I've missed so much time with him. I don't want to share. Everything you did—the bumps and bruises, the colds, the coaching—those are all things that I imagined doing one day. I'm not saying this is your fault. I'm thankful that Noah had you and that you were man enough to step up and play dad for a child that wasn't yours because not too many men will do that, especially considering the history between us. But this isn't up to me." He moves the ring on Josie's finger back and forth. She nods at him and mouths that she loves him.

Liam takes a deep breath. "Noah wants to see you. Most importantly, he wants you to coach his football and baseball teams. He didn't like his coach this year. In fact, I think the only one who did is Candy Appleton."

I can't hide my smile. Aubrey claps her hands before throwing them around my neck and giving me a kiss.

"I can see him?" The emotion is thick in my voice as I look at Liam, not Josie, for confirmation.

"I'm not going to deny my son because that would be wrong. You've been a part of his life for a long time and he has the right to continue a relationship with you if that's what he wants. But know this, Ashford: if you hurt my son again by disappearing for a year without a word, I'll hunt you down and make you pay. Am I clear?" Liam looks at me again. His gaze is deadly and I have no doubt he'd follow through with his threat. I know I screwed up and plan to do whatever Noah asks to make it up to him.

"Crystal," I say because other words escape me. I can't believe Liam just said I could see Noah. Not just see him, but coach him, as well. "Thank you,"I say, my voice cracking as I fight back the tears. I told myself I wouldn't cry, especially in front of Liam. I can't show him any weakness that he may want to exploit later.

Aubrey stands and pulls me into her arms. "I told you he'd be reasonable," she whispers in my ear. I pull her to me, burying my face in her neck and let out a long, ragged breath that I didn't know I was holding. I let her go all too soon, remembering our guests. She kisses me lightly on the cheek before turning back to Liam and Josie.

"Do you guys have time for coffee and dessert?"

Josie looks at Liam. He nods, which I know makes Aubrey's heart soar.

"Do you really want coffee, Westbury, or another beer?" I try the friendliness tactic, knowing it's a stretch.

Liam cracks a smile and shakes his head. "Beer."

"Coming right up." I gather up our plates and carry them to the kitchen. Aubrey is busy preparing dessert and coffee.

"Just you and Josie on the coffee."

"Okay, babe."

I take a moment and nuzzle into her neck. "I love you. Thank you for pushing me to do this. You'll love Noah. He's an amazing kid."

Aubrey turns and captures my lips, pulling away all too soon. "I can't wait."

Josie is piling napkins and gathering the bowls when I come back in. "What are you doing?"

"Helping," she says sheepishly. Liam shakes his head and takes the offered beer out of my hands.

"She does this all the time."

"Some things never change." My comment causes Liam to laugh. I join in when Josie shoots him a death stare. It's easy to see why they are meant to be together.

"Can I ask how Noah's doing?"

Aubrey comes in with a tray full of different cookies and slices of cake. She wanted to cook, be a hostess since they were coming over here, but with Josie bringing dinner she opted for the next best thing, even though they are store bought. It's the thought that counts, right? She sets the tray down and Liam reaches for a piece of cake while Josie takes her cup of coffee.

She lets it warm her hands before taking a sip and answering. "He's doing well. School is school. I don't think boys like school in general and he has a new friend that he hangs out with a lot who doesn't play football so that's nice." Josie speaks with pride. I miss that. I miss being able to brag about him.

"And are you guys together?" I ask, pointing to the both of them. Josie looks shocked when I ask, but I'm trying to be friendly. I honestly don't care and could ask anyone around town, but they're here.

"We are." It's Liam who answers. He's once again playing with her ring.

"Getting married soon?" I'm not bitter. She's been my friend for a long time. I care about her.

Josie looks over at Liam and it makes me wonder if she's doing the same thing to him that she's done to me. Avoidance. She's very good at it.

"Maybe next summer. We really haven't talked about setting a date and with the tour, things get crazy."

"Yeah I bet." I take a swig of my beer, as does Liam while Josie looks down at her cup of coffee.

"So Liam, Nick tells me that you're the lead singer of 4225 West."

Liam's face deadpans. He probably thought he was making it through dinner without talking about his alter ego. "I am. Are you a fan?"

"No, not really. I've heard a few of your songs though."

I try not to choke on my beer. Liam starts laughing, as does Josie. Aubrey sits there, perfect as a peach.

"Well I have to say, it's nice that I didn't walk into a fan-fest. When Josie told me we were coming over here, I just about freaked out. When I'm here I like being just Westbury, dad to Noah and

Josie's rocker, but some people don't see it like that. They bombard me all the time with merchandise to sign with promises to not sell it, only for it to end up on some auction site."

"Oh no, I don't need your autograph."

"Thank you." For the first time since Liam's been here his smile is genuine. Maybe there is hope for us to get along and be friends.

"How are Katelyn and the girls? I really miss them."

Liam sighs and shakes his head. Josie looks sad. My heart breaks for the Powell's.

"Katelyn is doing okay. She's managing and working for the band. Elle is doing fairly well actually, but Peyton, she has trouble sometimes," Josie says, holding in her emotions. I know her heart breaks for her best friend. I'll never forget that night when everything changed.

"That's expected. Are the girls talking to anyone?"

Liam shakes his head.

"Well, maybe now that I'm back, I can start seeing them and help them figure some stuff out."

"That'd be nice, Nick. You should let her know."

"I will, Josie, when I see her next time." Which I'm hoping is soon. "Um… I'm not trying to rush anything along, but when can I see Noah?"

"Tomorrow," they answer in unison.

"That's if you're not busy," Josie adds.

I look at Aubrey, who shakes her head. "No, we're not busy." I reply.

"Good, because he's driving us nuts. He knew you were back and has asked when he can see you. I do believe he wants to yell at you so be prepared. Either way, he knew we were coming over here and he wanted to come. As much as I hate saying this, my son missed you." Liam adds.

I can't hide my elation when they say tomorrow. I can't wait to see him. I can't wait to hug him and to apologize for my actions. I just hope he forgives me.

"I know this isn't what you want, but thank you."

"It's what Noah wants."

Knowing that I'll be seeing Noah tomorrow suddenly has me nervous. I know that Liam said he wants me to coach him, but what if after he meets Aubrey or doesn't like my excuse that he hates me? I don't think I can live with myself if he does.

Tomorrow is a new day.

Chapter 10

I stand on the football field and wait for school to get out. Noah is meeting me here. We were supposed to meet yesterday, but he wasn't feeling well. I won't lie, I was hurt and thought that he had changed his mind, but Josie assured me that he had eaten too much junk food the night before and was now paying the price. Something I remember him doing on occasion.

When I see him walking across the field I want to run and pull him into my arms. He's wearing a black beanie and his hands are tucked into his coat pockets. I'm glad to see he's not out in the cold without staying warm. I know telling him what to do is no longer my responsibility, but I'm not sure the doctor in me would be able to keep my mouth shut.

Noah looks up and sees me, and he starts to run. I can't keep my feet planted any longer. My stride is long and solid against the ground. His backpack is flopping from side to side as he pumps his arms back and forth, just as I taught him. I fall to my knees when we collide and hold him in my arms. His arms wrap around my neck and he squeezes me tight. I'm unable to fight the tears as they stream down my face. I was such a fool for leaving him. He didn't deserve the way I acted. I should've respected his choice in wanting to know his dad instead of making it difficult. I have so much to make up for.

Noah takes a shuddering breath and it breaks my heart to know that I've made him cry. I hold him tighter, hoping to show him that I'm here for him, that I'm not going anywhere.

"I'm so sorry, Noah."

He nods against my neck and all I can do is hold him and wait for him to be ready to talk. I don't know how long we stay in the field like this, but it's not nearly enough when he pulls back from me. He wipes his tears, his hands pulling down his cheeks. I don't know how many times Josie has told him not to do that, but he doesn't listen.

"I'm so mad at you."

"I know," I reply, swallowing the lump in my throat.

"Why did you leave me?"

As soon as he asks, his tears start flowing. I hate seeing him cry. I stand and pick him up and carry him over to the bleachers. He's so much heavier than I remember, but I suppose you forget the mundane things you've done for so long when you suddenly stop doing them. I know he's too big to be carried, but I'm doing it for me. I need him to know that I love him and that, regardless, he'll always be my boy.

I sit us down on the cold metal, wishing I had brought a blanket. I brought a football for us to throw around, not sure what to expect. Noah isn't an over-emotional child, but I think under the circumstances I will let him cry as much as he wants.

I hold him in my lap, much like I did when he was little and would come in crying because he scraped his knees. I'd patch him up and talk about being tough and the next time he fell, he fought the tears. Of course, Josie wailed enough for the both of them every time he'd come in banged up. If she'd had her choice, he'd walk around in bubble wrap.

Noah pulls back and slides off my lap, sitting next to me. He folds his hands in his lap and looks at me, waiting for my answer.

"I'm so sorry, Noah, for leaving the way I did. The only excuse I can offer is that I was angry with your mom and thought it would be best if I just left. I didn't think about how it would affect you."

"Why? Because of my dad?"

I shrug. "I thought that maybe you didn't need me anymore."

"But you're my dad, too. And you just left. I came home and you were gone. And you didn't answer your phone." His voice breaks, his lower lip starts to quiver.

I pull Noah into my arms and hold him tight. He wraps his arms around me as much as he can and sobs into my coat.

"How can I make it up to you?"

He pulls back and sniffs loudly, making me chuckle. He has little habits that Josie tries so hard to break and yet he still does them and it cracks me up.

"You want to make it up to me?"

I nod. "I do. I want to be a part of your life and your mom and dad said I can, but it's really up to you."

"I want you to coach my teams." He blurts out.

I can't help but smile. "Yeah, your dad said that. What's wrong with your new coach?"

Noah shrugs. "He didn't run the pass routes right and tried changing too much stuff and he let his son be quarterback and he can't even throw ten yards. The season was a mess and he says he's coaching baseball and I can't play for him anymore." Noah throws his hands up in the air, almost hitting me in the face. He's clearly frustrated with how things went this fall.

"I'd love to coach you. I honestly thought your dad would do it."

He climbs down from my lap and stands in front of me, dropping his backpack on the ground. "He wants to, but he gets busy. Maybe he can coach with you."

"Yeah, he could. He's pretty smart when it comes to quarterbacks." As much as I want to cringe, I can't. I won't. I refuse to cause any turmoil in his life. If he wants me to coach with Liam, I will.

"Are you going to stay?"

"I am. I'm not going anywhere. I promise."

Noah jumps into my arms. "I'm so glad that you came back."

"Me too, buddy." I play punch him in the stomach only for him to start shadow boxing with me. It looks like he's been practicing his moves. Not that I'd ever encourage him to box, but I hope he'd use the punching bag as part of his workout when he gets to high school.

Noah stops and sits back down next to me. He rests his legs out in front of him, copying my position, even crossing his ankles. "So what did you in Africa?"

"I helped a lot of kids when they got sick. I even helped deliver a couple of babies. I got to play football with some of the kids, but their football is our soccer. They can't afford to have helmets and pads to protect them."

"That's cool. I didn't do much while you were gone. I got to go on tour with my dad And we moved into his house." Noah shrugs and looks up at me.

"You can talk about your dad and living in his house. I'm okay with it."

His smile tells me that he needed this affirmation from me. "I have a new friend. His name is Quinn, but he doesn't play football or anything. His dad is Harrison and he's in the band with my dad."

"I can't wait to meet Quinn."

"You want to meet him?"

"Of course I do. I'd like things to be good between us. Just because your mom and I aren't together anymore doesn't mean our relationship has to change."

"Yeah," he says this so quietly I have to strain to hear him. He starts kicking the grass and looking across the field. I know something is going on in his little mind.

"What's wrong?"

Noah shakes his head. "Nothing, I just… I don't know what to call you because sometimes I used to call you dad. But I don't want my dad to get mad."

He shouldn't have to think about things like this. It's just a name, but I don't know the answer. Maybe it's something he should ask his dad and see how he feels about it.

"Have you asked your dad?"

"No. I didn't think you were coming back and now here you are."

"Fair enough, Noah. Why don't you ask your dad and get his thoughts. I don't care what you call me just as long as we get to hang out."

Noah's quiet for a few minutes as he stares off. I sit and watch him, hating the fact that I've missed a year. It's hard to believe that so much of his life was consumed in mine and I just walked away from him. I should kick my own ass.

"Mom said you got married."

I can't help but smile. I can't wait for him to meet Aubrey. "I did. Her name is Aubrey and she's very excited to meet you."

"Will I like her?"

"I hope so. When we picked out our new place, she mentioned you having a room there."

Noah turns to face me. His smile is wide and bright. "I have my own room?"

"If you want to come stay the night or need to stay, you're always welcome."

"Will this be like Junior Appleton when he has to go to his dad's house on the weekends?"

I shake my head. "No, we aren't sharing custody of you. I just get the liberty of having you visit."

"Cool. Thanks for wanting me," he says as he pulls me into a hug. I'm too choked up to respond. "Do you want to throw the ball around?"

Thank God for short attention spans. "Yeah, I do."

Noah and I head out to the field. He picks up the football and tosses it up in the air a few times. I stand about forty yards from him. This was the goal last year and if this new coach messed up his game, I'm going to have a lot of work ahead of me.

Noah steps into his three-step drop and fires. The ball falls short, going only twelve yards or so. I know he's young, but for his age he has a rocket. Seeing his face fall when his throw doesn't reach his target kills me.

I jog to the ball, pick it up and carry it over to him. His expression is pure defeat. I haven't seen him this way since we lost our last game. I set my hand on his shoulder and hand him the ball. He takes it reluctantly.

"What kind of game did you guys play this year?"

Noah sighs. "Mostly just a passing game. Any time we'd throw, he brought his son in."

This is why not just anyone should coach. You have to know the talent that you have and exploit it. Noah could throw and now he can't, which means his arm is out of shape.

"Tell you what. We can throw in the park across from your mom's shop after school as much as we can during the winter. We need to work on your arm and get it back in shape before baseball. You'll be fine, bud."

"Are you sure?"

"Yeah I am. I'm your coach, right?" I hold out my hand for a high-five.

Noah smiles and slaps my hand.

I head back out, but only about eight yards so we can play catch. We throw the ball back and forth until it's too dark to see. We walk back to the bleachers so he can get his backpack and head home.

"Want to come meet Aubrey?"

"Sure. I have to call my mom and ask."

"Yes, you do."

I walk forward, giving him a bit of privacy. He races to catch up with me, happy. "Mom said yes and said you have to feed me and help me with my homework."

I laugh as I get into truck. I hope that everything can be this easy. I know I have no say in how things go, but I hope that this will be an ongoing thing. Noah climbs in and shuts his door, happy that our night isn't over. He sings along to the radio and it's like nothing has changed, like the last year hasn't happened with the exception that he's coming over to my place to meet my wife.

Aubrey opens the door before I have a chance to turn the handle. Her hair is pulled back and she's wearing a Beaumont sweatshirt. When she sees Noah, her eyes light up. I kiss her cheek as we step into the loft. Noah looks around, setting his bag down in the chair.

"Noah, this is Aubrey. Aubrey, this is Noah."

Noah smiles and extends his hand. "It's very nice to meet you," he says politely. "My dad…um I mean Nick, 'cause he's my dad too, he smiles a lot when he talks about you."

"He smiles a lot when he talks about you, too. I'm very happy to meet you. I've heard so many great things."

Noah smiles and lets his eyes wander.

"I'll go start dinner."

"Thanks, babe." I watch her walk into the kitchen before giving Noah my full attention. "How about a tour and then we'll start some homework?"

I show Noah around the loft and let him take in the room that Aubrey made up for him today. I'm not sure if Josie and Liam will let him stay over, but if they do, I want to be prepared. I'm going to take whatever they are willing to offer.

"Your wife is really pretty."

"Yeah, she is. She's great. I think you'll like her a lot. She's very excited to watch you play baseball this spring."

"That'd be cool."

"Hey guys, dinner is on the table." Aubrey stands in the doorway, looking at Noah with a grin.

Noah and I follow her and sit at the table. Small talk is made, mostly between Aubrey and Noah. I love sitting there and listening to them as they get to know each other. Every so often Noah brings up something about me and his mom, but Aubrey is a champ and acts like it's no big deal. It shouldn't be a big deal; she's wearing my ring.

After dinner, Noah and I sit at the table and do homework. I don't miss these days. The curriculum has changed so much from when I was his age; they make it impossible for parents to help.

"Can I ask you a question?"

"Of course you can."

"Would you be mad if I changed my last name to Westbury?"

I wanted to adopt Noah more than anything. I wanted him to have my last name, but Josie was always hesitant. I knew she was always holding out hope that Liam would come back. I just didn't want to believe it. Noah has every right to carry his dad's last name whether I like it or not.

"I think your dad would like it if you did."

"Would you be mad?"

I shake my head. "No, Noah, I wouldn't be mad. Besides, I like the way Noah Westbury sounds. You should definitely change it." I wink at him.

Noah gets up and gives me a hug. "I'm really glad you're back. I missed you so much."

"I missed you too, bud."

I want to add that I'm never going away, but I think he knows that. From this day forward, I'm going to live my life with no regrets.

MY UNEXPECTED FOREVER

Coming Summer 2013

CHAPTER 2
Katelyn

I set the phone down, resting my head in my hands. I know I can do this. I just have to convince myself that Liam didn't make a mistake in hiring me. What was I thinking when I opened my mouth at Christmas saying I could be their manager? I fear I've bitten off more than I can chew, but Liam has confidence in me, even if I'm only booking 4225 West in small bars.

They laugh – the bar owners – when I call and book a gig. They ask if I'm joking and I assure them that I'm not. I tell them, repeatedly, that the band is trying a different angle, more family friendly and want to give back to the fans that have made them so popular. Still, I can hear the humor in their voices when they agree to a booking and the small fee is figured out. What they don't understand is with a bit of advertising they will clean house at the end of the night. 4225 West isn't asking for a large percentage; they just want to play and want to do it without the bright lights shining in their face.

My phone rings, startling me. I almost spill my coffee when I reach for the handset. My hand steadies the cup before there's a mess everywhere. I don't know where all these jitters are coming from... okay, yes I do. I know exactly what or who is setting me on edge. I just choose to ignore it. I can't focus on my children and career with the distractions that face me daily. I need to get through... I don't know what. He's my boss. That's what I keep telling myself, whether he's actually the one who signs my check or not. I work for him.

I pick up the phone on the fourth ring, clearing my throat and taking a deep breath before saying hello.

"Is this Katelyn Powell?"

"It is," I say, pulling my pad of paper closer to me to take notes.

"This is Christa Johnson and I represent an artist known as DeVon. He's an up-and-coming artist that we recently signed. His debut single releases next month and we're interested in getting him some attention. I'm calling to see if *4225 West* would be willing to work a small tour with him?"

"What type of music? He sounds more hip hop with a name like DeVon." I write down his name and scribble *research* next to it. I haven't heard of him, but that doesn't mean anything. When it comes to music, I'm pretty much in the clouds.

"You'd think, right? DeVon is actually blues with a rock vibe. It's very funky with a kick. We think that with the success of *4225 West*, DeVon will not only gain some fans, but will learn from the veterans and how they run a tour."

Veterans? I know I'm not a veteran when it comes to tours, but the guys are. Me? I'm just the person behind the desk trying to find places willing to pay them.

"Do you have venues set up?" This is important. How much work am I going to have to do?

"About fifteen, but we'd like thirty."

I can arrange the remaining venues. This will be good experience for me. "Where are you looking to tour?"

"Ideally, we'd like to hit the younger crowds, so Miami, New York City, Seattle."

"And when would you like to start?"

"We're hoping for August."

August? One month before school starts. Not that I need to be on tour with the guys, even though Liam will want me there. I'm sure Josie and Noah would go and Harrison would probably take Quinn as well. The guys have a new CD coming out and this would probably be a huge benefit for them. Thirty stops, is that enough?

"What about forty-five days?" I throw that number out there, hoping I'm doing the right thing. Liam has given me full reign to do whatever I see fit, but I still question everything. He rolls his eyes most of the time or tells me to ask Harrison and that's really not going to happen.

"We can do that."

"Great." Christa and I spend the next hour on the phone hashing out the details. I take copious notes and she promises to email the contacts from the venues she's already booked. We agree that I will take the lead as 4225 West will be the headliner.

I look out my window to see if the red studio light is still on. It's not. I gather my notepad and pen and head out to the studio. The guys are standing around Tyler, laughing. This is good. This means they've recorded something they like and are happy. I like happy.

Liam kisses me on the cheek when I walk up to him. He puts his arm around me, pulling me closer. He's been like this since he moved back. I'm not complaining. I love him like a brother and he's been there for us, helping out more than I could ever thank him for.

"Katelyn, did you meet Tyler?" Liam asks as he points to Tyler who nods.

"Yes, Jimmy brought him in to fill out his paperwork. Did you guys get something recorded?"

"No," Harrison says sharply. I look at him and immediately wish I didn't. He's staring at me, or Liam's hand. I'm not quite sure. Either way, his piercing green eyes are looking at me. His expression is stoic, almost hard.

"Well listen," I say. Liam drops his arms and moves so he's standing in front of me, leaving just enough space for the other guys to hear what I'm saying. We're talking business now; he's being serious. This Liam sometimes scares me. "I just got off the phone with a manager whose client is releasing a CD. His name is DeVon—"

"Is he a rapper?" Harrison asks, interrupting my spiel. I don't know why he does that, but it makes me want to slap my hand over his mouth.

I shake my head and continue. "DeVon is a blues artist with a bit of a rock kick. They're looking to build his fanbase and asked if we're interested in a tour. I figured with the CD about to come out, we could use the publicity so we're doing a forty-five-city tour starting in July. You guys will be back in time for the kids to start school."

"You guys?" Jimmy questions.

"Yes. I'll stay here."

"No, you'll be coming with us." Liam says. "Book a tour bus. Harrison can help. He has some connections and knows what we'll want. This will be fun."

Harrison and I stare at each other. The black beanie that he always wears is mocking my imagination of what his hair looks like. I've only seen him without his hat through pictures, never in person. I'm the first one to look away because I can't take the intense way he looks at me. Or maybe it's because I can't take the way I look at him. Or the way I want to know more about him.

Liam kisses me on the cheek before heading upstairs. He declares it's lunchtime before I have a chance to say anything. Jimmy and Tyler move faster than I've ever seen them before, leaving me with Harrison.

"Should we go into your office?"

I look up quickly, expecting him to smile or change his expression, but he doesn't. I remind myself that this is my job and he has the answers I need to get my job done; and as much as I don't want to sit in my office with him while he leans over me, it has to be done.

I nod and lead the way. I count the steps to my office and then to my desk; twenty, twenty-one, twenty-two. He pulls out my chair. I make the mistake of looking at him as I sit down. The slight turn of his lip tells me that he's happy to be here. He beat me into my office and I don't know how. Was I really walking that slowly?

He pushes in my chair slightly and leans over me. I try not to breathe in his cologne. I don't want to know what he wears, but he smells good. I lean away, closer to my screen and he leans in too. I wonder if he knows what he's doing to me. Doesn't he know I'm trying to avoid him? That we can never be anything?

Harrison tells me what site to bring up and I do. Except my fingers aren't working and I have to type the web address repeatedly. He moves his fingers over mine. I pull them back instantly, afraid for him to touch me. My hands rest in my lap.

"Sorry, I was just trying to help."

I nod and realize how stupid I'm being. We can be friends, right?

He brings up the website and walks me through how to order a custom charter. He says that they've used this company before and to call and ask for Larry; he'll make sure we get what we need and in time. I write down what he tells me and he laughs. I turn slightly, but think twice and focus on my paper.

"I think I can take it from here."

"Katelyn?"

The sound of his voice, the way he says my name, low and sweet with just enough mystery, makes me look up at him causing me to mentally kick myself.

"It's lunchtime and Linda doesn't like to leave out food for too long."

He's right. I slide my chair back. He moves one-step back giving me some space. I was hoping I could follow him upstairs, but he doesn't move or lead the way. He waits for me.

I feel stupid for feeling like this, but it's too soon after Mason. In fact, nothing will ever happen with Harrison. I know how he feels, but it just can't. Not only because I love Mason, but because he's not my type. I would never date a man who is covered in tattoos, wears a beanie and shorts all the time. He's the quintessential rocker and doesn't fit my life.

I don't care that the way he looks at me makes me feel wanted.

I don't care that the way he looks at me makes me feel desired.

I don't care that the way he smells makes me want to crawl into his skin until I'm enveloped in his scent.

I don't care because he's not Mason.

ABOUT THE AUTHOR

Heidi is the author of USA Today, Digital Book World, Amazon and Barnes & Noble Bestselling novel, Forever My Girl

Originally from the Pacific Northwest, she now lives in picturesque Vermont, with her husband and two daughters. Also renting space in their home is an over-hyper Beagle/Jack Russell and two Parakeets.

During the day Heidi is behind a desk talking about Land Use. At night, she's writing one of the many stories planned for release or sitting court-side during either daughter's basketball games.

OTHER NOVELS BY HEIDI MCLAUGHLIN

THE BEAUMONT SERIES

FOREVER MY GIRL

MY UNEXPECTED FOREVER - SUMMER, 2013

LOST IN YOU

CPSIA information can be obtained at www.ICGtesting.com
Printed in the USA
LVOW10s1702081013

356006LV00015B/638/P